Martin Bridge

In High Gear!

written by
Jessica Scott Kerrin

Illustrated by
Joseph Kelly

Kids Can Press

To Peter and Elliott, and to teachers like Connie Bourgeau
of Laurel Oak Elementary School in Naples, Florida, who read
Martin Bridge in their classes and make me feel a part of
something much bigger — J.S.K.

For Lise Laree Manning and Katya Brianne Manges.
And for Michael Patrick Manning, a zero-cool,
crackerjack supergenius and good friend — J.K.

Text © 2008 Jessica Scott Kerrin
Illustrations © 2008 Joseph Kelly

This is a work of fiction and any resemblance of characters to persons living or
dead is purely coincidental.

Kids Can Press acknowledges the financial support of the Government of Ontario,
through the Ontario Media Development Corporation's Ontario Book Initiative;
the Ontario Arts Council; the Canada Council for the Arts; and the Government
of Canada, through the BPIDP, for our publishing activity.

Published in Canada by
Kids Can Press Ltd.
29 Birch Avenue
Toronto, ON M4V 1E2

Published in the U.S. by
Kids Can Press Ltd.
2250 Military Road
Tonawanda, NY 14150

www.kidscanpress.com

Edited by Debbie Rogosin
Designed by Julia Naimska
Printed and bound in Canada

Interior art was drawn with graphite
and digitally shaded. Cover art was
painted with acrylic and pixels.

The text is set in GarthGraphic.

The hardcover edition of this book
is smyth sewn casebound.

The paperback edition of this book
is limp sewn with a drawn-on cover.

CM 08 0 9 8 7 6 5 4 3 2 1
CM PA 08 0 9 8 7 6 5 4 3 2 1

**Library and Archives Canada
Cataloguing in Publication**

Kerrin, Jessica Scott

    Martin Bridge in high gear! /
written by Jessica Scott Kerrin ;
illustrated by Joseph Kelly.

ISBN 978-1-55453-156-1 (bound)
ISBN 978-1-55453-157-8 (pbk.)

I. Kelly, Joseph II. Title.

PS8621.E77M364 2008   jC813'.6
C2007-902703-2

Kids Can Press is a *l*©**r**U**s**™ Entertainment company

Contents

Meet ...

Science Fair

"Who's on your team?" asked Martin's teacher, Mrs. Keenan, as she came around with her clipboard.

"Alex and Stuart," said Martin proudly. They were Martin's best friends. "And Laila," he added a little less enthusiastically.

Laila, who sat in front of Martin, had done her usual pushy thing, insisting that she be on their team.

"You four worked together the last time the class did group projects," said

Mrs. Keenan. "I'd like to change it up a bit." She consulted her clipboard. "Stuart," she directed. "Why don't you join *that* team?" She pointed to a threesome in the corner of the room. "And Gibson," she called out. Gibson looked up. "I want you to join this team over here."

Gibson? Martin frowned. He did not like losing Stuart from their group, but more than that, he was worried about the replacement Mrs. Keenan had assigned.

Gibson reminded Martin of Scoots, the notorious tabby cat who lived in their neighborhood. When Scoots wasn't getting stuck in trees or wedged under porches and having to be rescued by firefighters, the furry hazard liked to stroll across busy intersections, not even glancing at the cars that swerved in every direction.

Scoots was one lucky feline. And as far as Martin could tell, Gibson relied on luck, too.

"Okay, class," said Mrs. Keenan, after Gibson traipsed over and took a seat near Martin. "You now have your teams for the fair."

Martin's school held a science fair in the gym every spring. Last year, his class did solo projects, and he had presented his study of rockets. He would have gotten an A$^+$ if it hadn't been for that minor trajectory error and the overhead lights.

Martin shook his head at *that* shattering memory. He still felt everyone had overreacted.

Cripes!

"This year's theme is Save Our Planet," Mrs. Keenan continued.

Laila's hand shot up.

"I'll take questions in a minute," said Mrs. Keenan.

Laila reluctantly dropped her hand.

"So, for the rest of today's class, I want your teams to discuss what your project will be for this theme."

Laila's hand shot up again.

"Not yet, Laila," said Mrs. Keenan, crankiness creeping in.

Laila huffed a little as she tucked both hands into her armpits.

"And one more thing," said Mrs. Keenan warily. "I don't want projects that involve any type of trajectory" — she looked

directly at Martin — "exploding water balloons" — she looked directly at Laila — "or oozing slime" — she looked directly at Alex. "Any questions?"

Laila's hand did not shoot up. Instead, she bunched her pointy shoulders to her ears.

"Now, as I mentioned, your project is going to be about saving our planet," Mrs. Keenan continued. "But *this* year, it is also going to be about hard work and team effort."

Martin glanced over at Gibson.

Hard work? Team effort? These were not words that Martin would use to describe their newest member.

"And for that, your contribution will be recognized," said Mrs. Keenan. She began to dole out small blue cards. "Every group will receive twenty tickets. When your project is complete, you will decide, as a team, how many tickets each member will get."

Laila's hand shot up. "What if one person does *all* the work?" she demanded, protectively clutching the tickets that Mrs. Keenan had handed to her.

"Then they would get all twenty tickets. But only if everyone on the team agrees. However, if members contributed equally, then the team would divide the tickets evenly," explained Mrs. Keenan.

"What are these tickets good for?" asked Martin.

"That's the fun part," said Mrs. Keenan. "All the tickets will go into a basket, and I'll draw one name on the day of the fair. The prize for hard work and team effort will be a signed copy of Zip Rideout's special science edition comic book!"

15

"Ooooooooo!" chimed the class.

Martin practically whooped. Zip Rideout, Space Cadet, was his favorite cartoon superhero.

"So, does everybody understand the process?" asked Mrs. Keenan.

Heads nodded eagerly.

"Okay, then. You can begin your discussions."

The class shoved their desks into groups.

"Any ideas for saving our planet?" Martin asked over the classroom buzz.

"I have a few," said Laila with authority. She held up a long sheet of paper. Somehow, she had already produced a list.

"Hang on, Laila," said Alex irritably. "I have a few ideas, too!"

"Oh, *really?*" said Laila. "Like what?"

Alex fumbled around with the books on his desk, obviously buying time.

"Well," he said at last. "What about a beach walk?"

"A beach walk?" Laila laughed. "What does *that* have to do with saving our planet?"

"The beach is part of our planet, isn't it?" Alex demanded, red-faced.

Martin saw how he could come to his friend's rescue.

"You mean a beach walk where we go out and pick up litter, right?" suggested Martin helpfully.

Alex nodded. "Yes, that's what I mean. Exactly." He gave Laila a self-satisfied smile.

"I like it," said Martin.

Laila frowned as she checked her list.

"A beach walk might not be on *your* list," said Alex, arms crossed, "but it's still a good idea."

"Maybe," said Laila, tight lipped. She turned to Gibson. "What do *you* think?"

she asked in a last-ditch attempt to dismiss Alex and get back to her list.

"I say we go for a beach walk," said Gibson, ignoring Laila's blatant appeal.

As luck would have it, Mrs. Keenan swooped in to see how their team was doing just in time to hear Gibson's pronouncement.

"Great idea, Gibson! Well done!" she exclaimed. And before she could learn whose idea the beach walk actually was, she moved off to the next team.

Gibson shrugged sheepishly. Laila giggled at Alex's indignant scowl.

For the rest of the class, they worked out the details about when the beach walk would happen and what supplies they would need. But even with all that planning, something about Gibson's uncanny luck did not sit well with Martin.

And later, when Martin was out biking after school, he almost ran over Scoots. It cost him a scraped knee. He took this misfortune as a sign that Gibson was somehow going to cost him, too.

The next science class was spent talking about which beach they should clean up. Laila asked Gibson to take notes about their decisions, but he declined.

"I forgot my lucky pencil," he explained.

"Can't you write with something else?" asked Laila. "It's your turn, according to the schedule."

"What schedule?" asked Gibson.

"Glad you asked," said Laila, switching gears. She dug into her desk and pulled out copies of a detailed work schedule for the beach walk. It had color-coded tasks and deadlines and everything.

"That's a lot of tasks," said Gibson.

"Holy cow," said Alex.

Martin just whistled.

"Remember. This project is about hard work and team effort," Laila reminded them sternly.

Everyone mumbled in agreement. Then, after much debate, they chose Carter's Beach as their project destination. And Laila ended up taking notes.

Martin sat back and surveyed his team members. Laila had certainly done more than her fair share of the work today.

More tickets' worth than any of us, he thought.

And that's how it went for the next few weeks. Laila kept everyone organized, Martin and Alex struggled to keep up with their ever-increasing list of tasks, and Gibson lucked out, doing very little because grown-ups kept coming to his rescue.

"Look! The librarian had a special display on beaches," Gibson announced proudly, staggering under the weight of a stack of books that should have taken him hours to collect.

"Look! My mom's environmental group loaned me these protest signs," Gibson boasted as he lugged in placards to fulfill his task of making a backdrop for their display.

"Look! My uncle works in a radio studio, and he gave me this recording of whales singing that we can play during the science fair!" Gibson crowed in response to his sounds-of-the-beach assignment.

With each passing day, the team grew more and more frustrated. Gibson's luck was just too much to take, especially since the rest of them had to work so much harder to complete their own tasks.

Martin was the first to speak up.

"Mrs. Keenan," he said, standing in front of her desk after class was dismissed and Gibson had left the room. "Gibson isn't doing any work."

"Oh?" said Mrs. Keenan. "Didn't I see him bring in books on the beach? Protest signs? Whale songs?"

"Well ... sure," admitted Martin reluctantly.

"But he didn't do any work to get those," blurted Laila.

"He's just lucky that way," added Alex, to drive home their point.

"I see," said Mrs. Keenan.

Martin could tell from her tone that she didn't see.

"Have you told him how you feel?"

"Not exactly," muttered Martin.

"Then give that a try," offered Mrs. Keenan. "And if his tasks turned out to be easy, maybe he could take on a few more to even out the workload."

Encouraged, they marched out the door.

"Gibson!" Martin burst out the next time the team met, and Gibson had

breezed in without his lucky pencil once again. "You'll have to do some *real* work if you want to earn tickets and a chance for the prize!"

"What do you mean?" replied Gibson indignantly. "I've contributed plenty."

"You've contributed, all right," Martin replied. "But you've had plenty of luck.

We've had to work a lot harder than you to get our tasks done."

Alex nodded as back-up.

Gibson gave an unconcerned shrug.

"He's right, Gibson," said Laila, licking the tip of her red pencil and furiously revising her schedule. "Here's what you'll need to do to even out the workload."

She glowered at him, then spun her

schedule around so that everyone could see it.

Martin and Alex leaned forward, eager to learn what Laila had come up with.

"Stuart was our best printer," Laila continued, giving Gibson the gears. "Since we don't have him, you'll be in charge of making all the labels for our display board."

Whoa, thought Martin, sitting back.

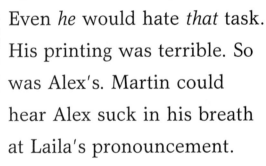

Even *he* would hate *that* task. His printing was terrible. So was Alex's. Martin could hear Alex suck in his breath at Laila's pronouncement.

"I'm not very good at printing," said Gibson. "The labels would take me a long time."

"Look, Gibson," said Laila icily. "This past weekend alone, Alex spent all kinds of time going to hardware stores to see if he could get donations of work gloves and recycling bags. Martin spent hours with his dad building those sticks we're going to spear the garbage with. And I passed on going to a matinee so that I could work on, well —" She paused to review her schedule. "— everything else," she concluded.

"Laila *is* way ahead on hard work and team effort," agreed Martin.

Alex nodded.

"Okay. No problem," said Gibson easily enough.

"He's up to something," grumbled Martin when Gibson left the room for a drink of water.

"I know!" said Laila, throwing her arms up helplessly. "But I can't think of anything else that would make him work like the rest of us."

"Well, if he doesn't do those labels, then I say he gets zero, that's *zero* tickets," Alex swore.

Laila nodded, but Martin hesitated. He actually felt a pang of sympathy for Gibson. The printing task was a hard one.

Martin certainly would not want to do it. But the pressure of both Alex and Laila staring at him made Martin nod in agreement, just as Gibson returned.

"I'm not sure I can make the beach walk on Saturday," said Gibson casually.

"What do you mean?!" demanded Martin. His pang of sympathy was instantly replaced by raw anger.

"I have to take care of Alice's pet hamster this weekend," explained Gibson, nonplussed.

Alice was a little girl in the neighborhood, and Martin had taken care of her hamster

many times when Alice's family went away.

"A hamster?!?" repeated Laila. There was poison in her voice.

"Yes. Named Ginny," said Gibson, as if this was the most reasonable explanation in the world. The rest of the team looked at one another in stunned amazement.

"You must be kidding!!" roared Alex.

Gibson blinked, unfazed.

"You're going on this beach walk, Gibson," insisted Laila, leaning forward menacingly.

"She's right," said Martin with a scowl. "Ginny's no work at all. So you're going to pick up garbage, just like the rest of us."

Alex stepped in and pointed his finger right at Gibson's chest. "And don't ..." *Jab.* "be ..." *Jab.* "late ..." *Jab, jab.* His words dropped out like stones.

Gibson shrugged in his laid-back way.

The bell rang, and everyone shoved their desks back into rows.

"I bet he doesn't show up for the beach walk," Martin lamented to Alex and Laila over lunch.

And, sure enough, Gibson didn't.

The team stood on the wind-whipped beach and waited a full fifteen minutes until Martin finally announced what was obvious to all: "He's not coming."

They spent the rest of the afternoon furiously spearing garbage along the shore and recording what they found. In the end, they collected four full bags. But making the beach pristine failed to lift their spirits.

On Monday, the team stormed into Mrs. Keenan's class in high gear.

"Gibson didn't do the beach walk," they complained in unison.

Mrs. Keenan looked up from her desk.

"Really?" she asked. "And you reminded him about the prize for hard work and team effort?"

"Yes," they griped together. "We did just

like you said."

"I see," said Mrs. Keenan calmly. "Perhaps I'll have a private word with Gibson. Are there still some important tasks that need to be done?"

"Labels," said Martin with vicious precision.

"Then I'll be sure to bring that to his attention," said Mrs. Keenan.

With some small satisfaction, they took their seats.

On the night before the science fair, the team met at Martin's house to put the final touches on their project. But there were still no labels.

"Where on earth is Gibson?!" demanded Laila, looking at her watch with wild eyes.

"I thought Mrs. Keenan had a word with him," Alex snarled.

Martin didn't say anything. He was too busy worrying about having to do those hateful labels himself.

As Martin's mom came in with a tray of milk and his favorite cookies, the doorbell rang.

It was Gibson. Everyone froze when he entered Martin's room.

"Sorry I'm late," he apologized. "I was

watching firefighters rescue Scoots from the top of a telephone pole."

There was no time for niceties.

"Did you print the labels?" Alex demanded.

"No," said Gibson, snatching a cookie from the tray.

Laila looked ready to scream.

"I brought this instead," said Gibson. He held up a label maker.

"Is that a label maker?" asked Martin.

"You said we needed labels, didn't you?" said Gibson, turning the machine on with one easy press of a button. He proceeded to pump out label after label and stick them onto their display board. He was done in ten minutes flat, and he *still* managed to eat most of the cookies.

"Got to go," said Gibson as he packed

up his label maker and brushed the crumbs from his face onto Martin's carpet. Out the door he went.

"The labels do look great," said Martin, finally breaking the silence.

"Yes, they do," admitted Alex. "But once again it took him no time at all. Meanwhile, I've spent *hours* on this project."

"*You've* spent hours," said Laila. "What about me?!"

"Okay, okay," said Martin, quick to intervene. "The project's done. Let's divvy up the tickets for hard work and team effort."

"There's twenty altogether," Alex reminded them while Laila pulled the blue cards out of her knapsack. "I say we give Laila seven. She did more work than

anyone. And I say Martin and I should get
six each."

"Sounds fair," said Martin, knowing
Laila would double-check Alex's math.

Laila counted out the tickets. "Wait a minute," she said. She held up a ticket. "There's one left."

"Really?" said Alex. He recounted on his fingers. "Well, you can't give it to Martin or me because we did the same amount of work."

"What about giving one more ticket to Laila?" suggested Martin.

"No," said Laila generously. "I didn't do *that* much more work than you two."

Silence.

"I guess Gibson gets it, then," said Martin at last.

Alex and Laila looked at him as if he were a traitor.

"Well, what else can we do with a single ticket? Besides, the labels do look great. And he also came through with the whale songs and protest signs and library books," Martin reminded them.

"I guess," said Alex grudgingly.

"It's only one ticket," admitted Laila with reluctance.

They filled their names in on the tickets, and Martin completed Gibson's for him.

The next morning, they dropped their tickets into the basket and set up their science project in the gym.

"Where's Gibson?" asked Mrs. Keenan when she came around to check on their progress.

"Who knows!" growled Alex. "We gave up on him."

Mrs. Keenan nodded sympathetically. She made a note on her clipboard before moving off.

Laila proceeded to neatly arrange a stack of handouts she had prepared on interesting ocean facts, a task that wasn't even on her list.

"Great work, Laila," said Martin sincerely, thinking she probably should have gotten that last ticket after all.

Laila beamed.

Gibson showed up moments later, once all the work was done.

"Lucky timing," said Martin testily.

Alex and Laila ignored him altogether.

"Attention, class," announced Mrs. Keenan from the stage. "I'm now going to draw the name for the prize for hard work and team effort."

Martin's heart did a little leap. He hoped his ticket would be picked. Sure, Laila had done more work, but because Martin was such a big Zip Rideout fan, he was certain the prize would mean more to him than to anyone else in the room.

"The prize goes to —" Mrs. Keenan plunged her hand into the basket of tickets, swirled them around, and pulled one out.

"— Gibson."

The crowd gasped.

Mrs. Keenan double-checked the ticket and cleared her throat. "Gibson," she repeated a little louder. "Come on up."

As Gibson wove his way through the crowd to claim his ill-gotten reward, there

was a slight smattering
of applause.

Alex wheeled
around. "How could
this have happened?"

Laila didn't say
anything at all. She just
kept staring straight
ahead, drop-jawed at
the unbelievable turn
of events.

Martin's ears burned as he watched
Gibson accept the Zip Rideout comic book.

"I thought you said Gibson hardly did
any work," said Mrs. Keenan when she
visited their project later on. Gibson was
busy wandering around the science fair,
showing off his prize.

"He didn't," said Alex with open
hostility. "Gibson's just plain lucky."

"You're absolutely right," agreed Mrs.
Keenan. "And he was especially lucky to
have been placed with such hard-working
classmates. You three have done an
excellent job."

The team mulled this over as Mrs. Keenan posted their mark on their display.

An A^{++}.

"*Two* plusses! said Laila in awe.

"Holy cow!" exclaimed Alex.

"Thanks, Mrs. Keenan!" said Martin. He felt as if he would burst.

Martin and Alex play-punched each other in the shoulder, and Laila gave them both little hugs.

"Gibson will get his own mark," said Mrs. Keenan, and she moved off to score the rest of the projects.

The next time Martin spotted Gibson was on the school bus ride home.

"Just look at Gibson," said Martin dryly to Stuart, who sat beside him. "He's *still* riffling through  Zip's fabulous space adventures."

"Gibson's lucky, all right," agreed Stuart. "But *you* got an A with double plusses! Congratulations on the top mark at the fair!"

"Well, thanks!" said Martin. "We worked hard." He was surprised to discover that receiving two plusses still made him smile.

Beam, in fact.

The bus pulled up to Gibson's stop.

Martin watched Gibson hastily jam his lucky prize into his knapsack and jump off. But as the bus pulled away from the curb, something fluttered by the window and caught Martin's eye. He elbowed Stuart and turned around in his seat to peer out.

There was Gibson chasing his wind-blown comic book down the sidewalk. It stopped only when it landed in a monster-sized puddle. He bent down to retrieve the

sopping mess just as Scoots rocketed past, a rambunctious dog in hot pursuit.

Gibson got soaked. Twice.

It was hilarious!

"That's the thing about luck," said Stuart with a shrug. "It comes and goes."

"But an A with double plusses stays put," concluded Martin. He heaved a contented sigh and settled in for the rest of the ride.

Bicycle

Martin heard the dull thump of suitcases being set down on the driveway, so he knew he should finish up in the garage.

Instead, he continued his attempts to un-jam the gears on his bicycle, while trying to ignore the disconcerting sounds.

"Martin," his mom sang out. "Aunt Laverne has arrived."

"Be right there," Martin replied as politely as he could muster.

At dinnertime only two days earlier, he

had been told that Aunt Laverne would be coming for a three-week visit. Martin could barely finish his chocolate pudding when he heard *that* unhappy news.

Aunt Laverne was really Martin's great-aunt on his father's side. But there was nothing great about her.

Aunt Laverne was the kind of aunt who did things only when she wanted to. Her voice sounded all rusty. And she had blue hair the color of lawn-mower smoke. Even worse, Aunt Laverne always seemed to be wagging

her knobby finger at Martin whenever she
came for a visit.

Aunt Laverne was not Martin's favorite
family member.

Martin sighed, then
trundled into the house.

"Hello, Aunt Laverne,"
he said, dutifully giving
her a hug. Her thick
lavender perfume
almost made
him choke.

"Hello, Martin," returned Aunt Laverne. "You've grown," she added, like an accusation.

It was true that Martin and Aunt Laverne were almost the same height. Either Martin had shot up, or Aunt Laverne had shrunk, the way old people do.

"What's that on your hands?" she demanded, interrogation-style.

"Grease," said Martin apologetically. "I was trying to fix my bike."

"Martin's bike keeps breaking down," explained his dad. "As soon as there's a good sale, we've promised him a new one."

"Kids these days get way too much," grumped Aunt Laverne, shaking her head in disgust. "They need to learn a thing or two."

"Come. Let's sit down," said Martin's mom cheerily as Martin's dad helped Aunt Laverne with her coat and hat and matching purse.

Martin dawdled in the front hall, hoping he could slip back to the garage unnoticed.

But no such luck.

"Martin!" his mom called from the sofa.

Cripes!

Martin sighed audibly, then joined

them, flopping down on the armchair nearest the escape route. He sat in agony while the grown-ups had a terrifically boring conversation that had nothing to do

with him. It went on forever.

"You should sit up properly, Martin," barked Aunt Laverne at one point. "Posture is important for a growing boy."

Martin grudgingly sat up straight.

"You're slouching again," Aunt Laverne nagged moments later, interrupting his misery once more.

And that was exactly the kind of nit-picking that went on for the next few days.

"Cut your meat into smaller pieces."

"Did you comb your hair? You missed the back."

"Is that your coat on the floor?"

Martin tried to get away by playing outside. But as often as not, she would follow him. Then Martin's ears would burn while she told the garbage collectors

not to dent the trash cans, and the postal worker not to be late again with the mail, and the paper carrier not to fling the newspaper onto the porch.

"These people need to learn a thing or two," complained Aunt Laverne.

Fortunately, Aunt Laverne could not climb ladders. So Martin found himself spending more and more time in his tree fort.

Then one morning, Martin looked out of his bedroom window and spotted his dad wheeling Martin's bike to the curb and leaving it there. What was he doing?!

Martin flew down the stairs to find a shiny new bike in the front hall.

"Surprise!" his mom called as she and Martin's dad hurried in, all smiles.

"For me?!" gasped Martin. He ran his hand over the cushiony seat and racy

handlebars, then crouched down, eager to examine every detail.

"You bet, Sport! The bike shop finally had their big sale," Martin's dad explained.

Martin jumped up and hugged both his parents.

"Thanks, Dad! Thanks, Mom!"

He climbed on the bike to get a feel for the ride.

"What's that bike doing in the house?" demanded Aunt Laverne in her rusty voice as she flapped down the stairs in her gray felt slippers.

"This is Martin's new bike," said Martin's dad proudly. "The only thing that worked on his old one was the lock!" He pointed to Martin's lock and chain wrapped around the new bike's seat stem.

"What does he need with a fancy bike

like that?" she said, wagging her knobby finger. "You're spoiling this child."

"Can I take it for a ride?" asked Martin, ignoring her dire warnings.

"Of course," said his mom. "In fact, why don't you run an errand for me at the mini-mart and pick up a few items for breakfast."

"Sure thing," said Martin, delighted to help out.

"We need eggs, coffee cream, dish detergent and raspberry jam," she said as she handed him some money. "Oh, and brown sugar." She paused. "Do you want me to write this down?"

"No, I've got it," said Martin, feeling very grown-up. "Eggs, coffee cream, dish detergent and raspberry jam."

"And brown sugar," reminded his mom.

"Right," said Martin. "Brown sugar," he repeated.

Martin grabbed his helmet and knapsack. "Onwards and upwards," he said, giving them the official Zip Rideout salute.

Martin wheeled his bike past Aunt Laverne, who stood clucking her tongue, and right on out the front door. After a few

initial wobbles, he quickly settled into the steady rhythm of pedaling up the street.

Then he tested everything. The brakes. The shocks. The gears.

He even got to try the bell when Scoots, the neighbor's cat, dashed in front of him. The bike worked perfectly!

All too soon, Martin pulled up to the mini-mart. He carefully locked his bike to the rack so as not to scratch the pristine paint job.

Once inside, Martin picked up a basket and tried to concentrate. What was on that list again?

Eggs for sure. And then there was something for toast. Butter? Honey? Butter. He was quite certain. And something about coffee.

Martin went to the coffee aisle and was overwhelmed. There were so many different types! Decaf sounded fancy, so he put that in his basket.

He walked right by the dish detergents, instead adding a box of laundry soap to his

purchases. And he completely forgot about sugar of any color.

Martin marched confidently to the check-out counter. The clerk rang his items through, and Martin loaded the groceries into his knapsack. He couldn't wait to

jump back on his new bike for the glorious ride home.

Martin charged out the door in high gear. But when he got to the bike rack, he stopped dead in his tracks.

Where was his bike?

Confused, Martin checked the entire rack. His new bike was definitely not there.

Martin whirled around, heart pounding, and frantically scanned in every direction.

All he saw were
customers going in and
out of the mini-mart,
some pushing shopping
carts, others loaded
with heavy bags.

But his bike was
nowhere to be seen.

Martin broke
into a frenzied run,
dodging back and forth
across the parking lot,
around the rear of the
store, and up and down
the street. His bike had
to be somewhere!

It *had* to be!!
But it wasn't.

At last, Martin doubled over, gasping to catch his breath.

When he recovered, he walked stiffly to the rack where he *knew* he had secured his bike. He bent down and scooped up the chain for his lock. It had been cut in half.

With awful certainty, Martin came to

the obvious, terrible conclusion. His bike
had been *stolen*.

The bike he had so carefully locked up.
The bike he had gotten to ride only once.
The bike his parents had taken so long to
save up for.

Anger flared. Who could have done this?
Who would steal a kid's brand-new bike?
And why wasn't anyone in the parking lot
paying attention?

But anger quickly gave
way to crushing sadness.

My poor bike, thought
Martin, hanging his head.
He would have taken such
good care of it.

"I'm so sorry," he
whispered to the space

where his beautiful bike had once been.

Martin trudged home.

"What's wrong?" asked his mom when she came to the door. She was smiling at first, but then looked alarmed when she saw Martin's expression.

"My bike was stolen," Martin croaked. His throat was so tight, he had trouble speaking.

"What?! No!" exclaimed his mom, one hand on Martin's shoulder, the other over her mouth.

"What's going on?" asked Martin's dad, who had come to the door.

Aunt Laverne was close behind.

Now Martin's throat was so clenched, he couldn't say anything at all. Instead, he stared at the ground with watery eyes.

"He says his bike was stolen," said Martin's mom in a hushed voice.

Martin braved a glance at her. Her eyes were filling up, too.

"What did I tell you!" Aunt Laverne barged in. "That bike was way too extravagant for a boy his age. You parents need to learn a thing or two!"

"Not now, Aunt Laverne," said Martin's dad crossly.

It was the first time Martin had ever heard his dad challenge her.

"Well!" exclaimed Aunt Laverne, and she huffed back inside.

"Did you forget to lock your bike, Sport?" asked Martin's dad gently.

"No, Dad. I didn't." Martin dug out the chain from his knapsack as proof.

His dad inspected the evidence. "Bolt cutters," he muttered.

"Oh, Martin," said Martin's mom, giving him a hug.

Martin gulped hard.

"I better get breakfast started," said Martin's dad sadly, and he took Martin's knapsack into the kitchen.

Martin said nothing. He plunked down
on the front steps, knowing that it was
going to be a long time before his
parents could save for a bike
again. His mom sat
down beside
him.

After a few bleak moments, Martin's dad returned with the keys to the van.

"Where are you going?" Martin's mom asked.

"The mini-mart," said Martin's dad. "There are a few more things we need."

Breakfast, when it finally came, was a glum affair. Everyone poked at their eggs, lost in thought over the morning's tragic events.

It was Aunt Laverne who finally broke the silence.

"Someone in a truck picked up Martin's old bike from the curb this morning," she remarked. "And it wasn't the regular garbage collector."

"Really," said Martin's dad, barely looking up.

"So I demanded to know what he was doing. It turns out that he was taking it to a place that makes new bikes from old ones."

"Oh, I've heard of it," said Martin's mom. "The shop is run by a retired police officer. He rescues broken bikes that would be going to the dump, salvages the working parts and builds new bikes out of them. And then he gives those bikes to kids from families in need."

"Maybe you should go there," said Aunt Laverne to Martin, "and see if the shop can help you build a new bike. Then you'll learn a thing or two."

Martin scooped up the last bit of his eggs, mulling this over. He liked tools. He liked fixing things. And rebuilding his old bike would definitely be better than having no bike at all.

"What's the place called?" Martin asked.

"Bicycle Recycle," said his mom. "Or something like that."

"Can we go after breakfast, Dad?" asked Martin.

"Sure, Sport," said his dad. "It wouldn't hurt to check out the place."

"I'm coming, too," said Aunt Laverne.

And because of Martin's fledgling new hope, for once he didn't mind her tagging along.

The next thing Martin knew, he was sitting in the van, holding a piece of paper with Bicycle Recycle's address written on it.

"There," said Aunt Laverne, pointing with her knobby finger. "That looks like the place."

Martin was disappointed at what he saw. The big sign in the window was hand-made, and the building itself was rather shabby. The steps to the door were crumbling. The outdoor light fixture was missing its shade.

"Are you coming, Sport?" asked
Martin's dad as he slid open the van door.

Aunt Laverne was already climbing the
front steps.

Martin nodded reluctantly and undid
his seat belt.

Once inside, Martin was surprised to find Aunt Laverne in high gear, chatting with the man behind the counter.

"That's my sister's grandson," remarked Aunt Laverne, scarcely glancing Martin's way.

"Hi. My name's Darby," said the man in a deep voice, and he came out from behind the counter to shake Martin's hand.

Darby's hands were huge, and he was practically bald, except for a few tufts of hair behind his ears.

"So, you're a police officer," said Martin's dad.

"*Retired* police officer," Darby corrected him.

"What made you get involved in this?" asked Martin's dad, nodding at the shop.

"When I was on the beat, I saw a lot of poverty. Kids with nothing to do. No parks to play in. No bikes."

Martin nodded sympathetically. He remembered all the times he had ridden around his neighborhood park, having one adventure after another with his two best friends. And now, he didn't have a bike.

There was nothing worse.

Just then, a creaky pick-up truck filled with bikes pulled into the parking lot. Martin could see that many of the bikes were twisted and rusty beyond hope.

"You fix *those?*" said Martin in awe.

"Not just fix," said Darby. "I rebuild."

He ducked into the back room and came out wheeling a shiny bike, complete with training wheels.

"It looks brand-new, but this bike is made from the parts of about six others," said Darby proudly. "And all my bikes get paint jobs. I build three or four a week, and when they're ready,

I call the agency. They send the kids over to pick up their bikes. The kids on the agency's list are pretty special," he added.

The truck driver started to unload the bikes, and Martin spotted something familiar.

"You were right, Aunt Laverne! There's my old bike!" Martin turned to Darby. "Do you think I could have my old bike back and you could help me rebuild it?"

"Well, sure," said Darby. "But first I've got to build bikes for the kids on my list."

"What if I helped you build some?" offered Martin, thinking that if he did, it would speed things up a bit.

"Volunteer? Great! How about you help out on Saturday mornings for the next couple of months?"

Martin nodded vigorously.

The next Saturday, Martin reported for duty just as a truckload of cast-off bikes arrived.

"Come outside and help unload," said Darby.

They brought the bikes into the shop, and Martin watched carefully as Darby disassembled them. Martin got to know the names of all the parts, and then he took his old bike apart himself and sorted the pieces into bins.

"Front forks here. Calipers there. Cranks over here. Shift levers in there. Derailleurs here," he recited proudly.

After a couple of Saturdays, Martin could hand the correct tools to Darby as he needed them. And it was always fun to be

the first to see the bikes when they came out of the paint booth in the back room. The finished bikes were masterpieces.

Best of all, Martin loved watching Darby give the bikes away. Eager kids would burst through the door, and after Darby checked their names on his clipboard, he would wheel out bike after shiny bike. The kids were thrilled.

"But Darby never wants anyone to make a fuss over thanking him," reported Martin back at home over dinner. "Darby's the best."

Later that evening, Martin stood at the doorway of the guest room.

"Aunt Laverne," said Martin. "Thanks for telling me about Bicycle Recycle."

"Darby does good work," said Aunt Laverne gruffly.

She was packing her suitcases. She stopped what she was doing and turned to Martin.

"I wished I had a bike, growing up," she said in a voice a little less rusty than usual. "But I never got one."

"That's sad," said Martin, remembering Darby's words about the kids he'd seen on his beat.

"I never had a lot of things. You're one lucky boy," she added, back to her old rusty tone.

Martin nodded. He returned to his own room, wondering what Aunt Laverne might have been like if she had gotten her childhood wish.

Aunt Laverne left the next morning.

"This flight better be on time," she warned the ticket agent at the airport, nit-picking to the end. "Your pilots need to learn a thing or two."

Weeks went by, and Martin showed up faithfully at Bicycle Recycle every Saturday. He was becoming quite a pro at the job. Darby even cleared a space so that Martin could have his very own workbench.

Then one Saturday, Darby stopped what he was doing and turned to Martin. "This bike we're working on includes parts from *your* old bike. How about we say this one belongs to you when it's finished, and you can have it on your last day here?"

"Really?" exclaimed Martin, his heart leaping.

Darby nodded to confirm.

All week Martin talked excitedly about getting his new bike. Because he had helped work on it, this bike somehow felt even more special than the one that had been stolen.

When Martin arrived at Bicycle Recycle for his last day, there was already a family waiting.

Darby checked his clipboard to see if their name was on the list, and then handed over a lime-green bike with purple racing stripes to a boy a few years older than Martin. The boy whooped repeatedly as he eased the bike out the door.

Later that morning, another family arrived. A girl in pigtails squealed in delight when Darby presented her with a tiny bike on training wheels. She especially liked the wicker basket on the handlebars and shoved her teddy bear in it for a ride.

The last bike to be handed out went to a family with two boys. The older brother

had received a bike a few months back, but he was there to share his younger brother's excitement.

"I really love my bike," he told Darby. "My little brother can't wait to get his."

Out came a red bike with gold flecks in the paint.

"Wow!" said the younger brother, all eyes.

Darby beamed.

After they left, he turned to Martin. "Well, I guess you're ready to see your bike now."

Martin nodded eagerly.

Darby returned to the back room and came out wheeling a gorgeous blue bike with flame-orange decals.

"It's perfect!" exclaimed Martin.

"You've been a great help," said Darby, patting Martin roughly on the back.

Martin was so pleased, he couldn't speak.

Just then, a boy about Martin's age burst into the shop, his dad tagging along behind.

"See, Dad! We made it!" shouted the boy.

"Truck broke down," explained the dad with a tired shrug. "Didn't think we'd get here in time."

The boy rushed over to Martin's bike.

"Is this it?!" the boy exclaimed, pulling the bike right out of Martin's hands. "Look, Dad, look!"

Martin didn't know what to say. He glanced at Darby, who was busy flipping through papers on his clipboard.

"Is your name Cameron?" Darby asked kindly.

"That's me!" said the boy, practically hopping.

"I'm sorry, son," said Darby, "but you're on the list for getting a bike *next* week."

"*Next* week," the boy repeated in a little voice as his face collapsed.

"I'm so sorry," Darby repeated, his booming voice reduced to a whisper.

The boy reluctantly let go of the bike

and stood staring at the ground, blinking hard, hands shoved into his pockets.

Martin could tell that this was a boy who didn't get a lot of things.

Just like Aunt Laverne, when she was young.

"I think you'd better recheck your list," Martin said to Darby, "because I'm pretty sure this one *is* Cameron's bike."

The boy raised his head, hardly daring to believe Martin's words.

"Really?" he asked.

Martin nodded, and the boy hugged him fiercely. Then he took hold of the bike and wheeled it over to his dad, who ran his hand over the frame in a way that Martin could tell was deeply grateful.

Martin and Darby watched proudly as

the bike was lifted gently into the back of
their old truck.

"Think you can help out one more
Saturday? I'll have a really nice bike for
you then," said Darby.

"That'd be great," said Martin.

"Why'd you do it?" asked Darby. "Give that bike away?"

Martin shrugged with immense satisfaction. For just as Aunt Laverne predicted, he *had* learned a thing or two.

Jessica Scott Kerrin, who lives in Halifax, Nova Scotia, loves detailed schedules with color-coded tasks. In her free time, she enjoys beach walks along her province's pristine coast. She also shares a tandem bike with her husband and once borrowed her son's  scooter to get to work when she had a flat tire.

 **Joseph Kelly** often asks his wife, son and daughter to pose for the drawings of the characters in Martin's world — Martin, his friends, Zip Rideout, and sometimes even space aliens! Now Byron, the family cat, who curls up and snores beside Joseph while he draws, has been immortalized as a model for Scoots. Sonoma, California, has a new star!

Darby's Tips on Keeping Your Bike Safe

Parking your bike:

Find a tall pole and rest your bike seat against it. Then back-pedal the pole-side pedal until it comes up (to about 12 o'clock) and touches the pole. Ta-da! The concave shape of the seat keeps your bike from rolling forward, and the pedal keeps your bike from rolling backward. Your bike won't fall over and get dinged and dented and is now ready to be locked.

Locking tips:

Don't lock your bike to something weak, such as a small tree or a chain link fence. Make sure your bike cannot be stolen by being lifted over what you have locked it to. Using two different types of

locks, such as a horseshoe lock and a cable lock, makes your bike harder to steal. And don't lock only one wheel of your bike; lock the frame, too.

Serial number:

Always record your serial number to give to the police in case of theft. Most bicycle serial numbers are located on the underside of the bottom bracket near the pedals (you may need to turn your bike over to find it). That's your bike's fingerprint!

Catch up on all of Martin's adventures!

"Realistic, everyday situations, likable characters and simple stories written in rich language with solid dialogue and humor ... readers will eagerly anticipate every new installment." — **Kirkus Reviews**

HC ISBN: 978-1-55337-688-0   HC ISBN: 978-1-55337-689-7   HC ISBN: 978-1-55337-961-4
PB ISBN: 978-1-55337-772-6   PB ISBN: 978-1-55337-773-3   PB ISBN: 978-1-55337-962-1

HC ISBN: 978-1-55337-976-8   HC ISBN: 978-1-55453-148-6
PB ISBN: 978-1-55337-977-5   PB ISBN: 978-1-55453-149-3

PB $4.95 US / $5.95 CDN   •   HC $14.95 US / $16.95 CDN
$5.95 US / $6.95 CDN

Written by Jessica Scott Kerrin   •   Illustrated by Joseph Kelly